T0128444

Menopause is Maddening.

Written by Debbie Roth

Illustrated by Gabrielle Godino

Menopause is Maddening

iUniverse books may be ordered through booksellers or by contacting:

iUniverse
1663 Liberty Drive
Bloomington, IN 47403
www.iuniverse.com
844-349-9409

ISBN: 978-1-6632-2446-0 (sc)
ISBN: 978-1-6632-2447-7 (e)

Library of Congress Control Number: 2021912287

Print information available on the last page.

iUniverse rev. date: 06/18/2021

Menopause is Maddening.

Written by Debbie Roth
Illustrated by Gabrielle Godino

If you give a woman
a glass of wine...

The story of menopause
as told in rhyme.

This book is not for those
who easily scare,
but if you're not yet in menopause
it'll help you prepare!

If you're the type
who is timid and shy,
the blunt honest truth
may make you cry.

This tale has actually
been written multiple times,
but not because
I'm lacking in rhymes.
Each time the notes
have been misplaced,
my menopausal memory
has left me disgraced.

It's usually a slow
            insidious start.

A tiny sneeze becomes
an embarrassing fart!

You laugh too hard
            and spring a leak,

and think, "Oh no,
            I've passed my peak!"

The bed used to be a
place for sex and sleep,
but now its a place
to sweat and weep.

If your partner's a woman she'll
understand the situation,

but the bed will be soaked with
twice as much perspiration!

For you, sleep is a luxury
that's obscure and elusive.
Anyone who dares to wake you
may trigger behavior
that's abusive.

Your husband of course
is still in his prime
so he'll want to have sex
just about all the time!

But your body and mind
are in a different place,
which should make him
think twice before
invading your space.

The hot flashes are
powerful, your skin's
embarrassingly red
and you feel it intensely
from your toes to
your head.

You'll find most of your
body is now bathed
in sweat,
except that one special
spot that's dry when you
wish it was wet.

So even though it is
snowing and everyone's
turning up the heat,
you're sleeping naked,
barely covered by a sheet.

Somehow you're still
sweating despite the
fan overhead

and your partner's dressed
like an Eskimo when he
gets into bed.

Your body now has
a new type of inflation,
they say it is part of this
new maturation.

Suddenly your boobs
are hanging straight
down to your knees,

and your neck and your
stomach now look like
Swiss cheese.

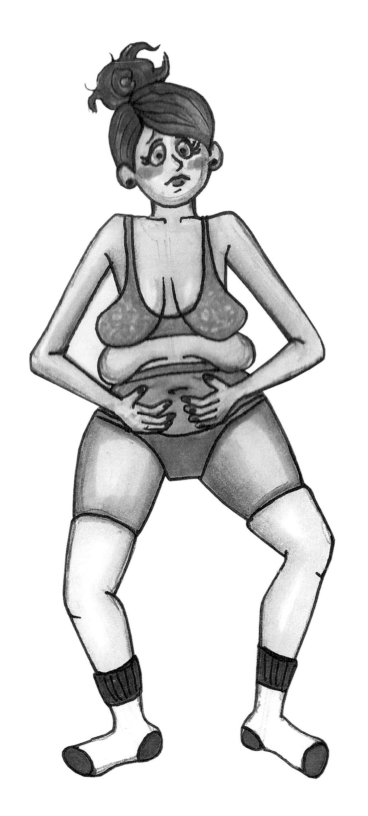

Your ass starts to jiggle
your belly can't be
contained,

even though you could
swear your weight hasn't
changed!

The lump seems to settle
in the middle of
your frame,

causing an unsightly bulge
that you just cannot tame!

You tighten the bra and
hoist up the girls,
now the back fat becomes
rows of endless swirls.

Suddenly someone's
shrunk the print on
all your devices

and your eyes are
so swollen
they're covered in
cucumber slices.

You buy readers and stash
them throughout the
house and the car,
but somehow you just never
know where they are!

When you finally find them
and they're all in one place
a look of horror suddenly
appears on your face.

You put on the glasses, your
vision's now clear as can be,
but you no longer remember
what you were trying to see!

This menopause phase may
have your husband confused,
but sometimes it seems like
your kids are amused.

"Look out my daughters!"
is what you should say,
"Cause this menopause shit
is coming your way."

To the men who live their
lives in ignorant bliss,
it's best to shut up and give your
wife a kiss.

Unless that's not what she wants,
which you may not know...
So at the first sign of rage you
should probably go!

And if you live with someone
in this phase of life:
be it a mother, a sister or
especially a wife...
Start apologizing now, accept
blame for each accusation;
any excuse you make will add to
your incrimination.

So be patient, be gentle,
be tolerant, be kind.

It's only temporarily that
she's lost her mind.

And if you put a straw in
her favorite bottle
of wine…

Maybe she'll no longer
think you're a swine.

Now that you're in this
menopausal phase
it seems you may have
to adjust your ways.

Getting younger is not
likely a choice,
so now you'll need to
use your voice.

Tell everyone
both near and far
in what phase of life
you currently are!

Warn them that your
moods will easily shift
and hope this warning
will prevent a rift.

Be sure to make the most of
this phase of the journey
because you really don't want
to end up on a gurney.

By now you know what
matters most in life
and you've surely learned how
to avoid the strife.

This is your time to have fun;
go ahead, spread your wings.

Take advantage of your
freedom and try some
new things!

Printed in the United States
by Baker & Taylor Publisher Services